Best wishes
Brie
x

Magic still exists
in special places
- if you know
how to find it!

Hope Hamlet,
in the South
West of England,
is one of
those places...

Hope Hamlet

Hope School

Mr. Bunn's Baker

Market

Land of the sheeps

Afternoon Tea House

Phyllis's House
Blue Flower Shop
Marco's Carpentry Shop
Shady Woods
Park
Vivien's Gallery
Valley of the Cows
Thirsty Moos Milk Shop
Bank
Mrs. Ghana's House
Rainbow Libra

Siggy Loves Sausages

First published in 2021.

Written by Brian Frederick
Illustrated by Vivien Sárkány
Page design by Bryony van der Merwe

ISBN: 978-1-7399064-0-5 (hardcover)
ISBN: 978-1-7399064-1-2 (paperback)
ISBN: 978-1-7399064-2-9 (mobi eBook)
ISBN: 978-1-7399064-3-6 (epub eBook)

Published by
BIBA BOOKS, LTD.
Bristol, United Kingdom
https://bibabooks.com

To: my wonderful
Harvinder,
my spirit and soul.
For: Sreyda, Hetty, Phoebe and
Daiya, with much love xxx
Thanks: to Maggie, Rachel,
Mike n' Barb, Linda and
all you good, good people.
You know who you
are xxx

Sigmund the dachshund

lived in the little hamlet of Hope in the English county of Somerset.

He lived with Phyllis and her mum and dad at No.16 Watercress Lane.

When he was a little puppy, Phyllis had been very young too and wasn't able to say Sigmund, so she called him Siggy, and that's been his name ever since.

One very windy day,

Siggy heard a loud commotion outside.

When he went to investigate, he saw a most wondrous thing. It floated in the air, white and sparkly, with brilliant red and gold patterns.

It was an expensive paper bag from a fancy ladies' boutique.

It swooped and soared and blew about in the wind.

Siggy was transfixed.
He was fascinated.

Then he saw Mrs Chana nearby.
She looked upset.

"Oh no! My bag!" she cried.
"Help me! It's my daughter's surprise birthday present!"

She clutched at the empty air as the bag swirled above her.

Siggy watched as a great gust of wind caught the bag, taking it even higher and then rocketing off into the distance.

"Don't worry, Mrs Chana!" called Siggy. "I'll catch it for you. I promise!"

Then off he **zoomed** after the bag.

He chased it down the lane, around the corner,
and into the village marketplace.

Siggy galloped past Mr Bunn, the baker, who was opening his shop.

A lovely smell wafted out of the door.

Siggy looked back at him as he raced on, and said,
"Sorry, Mr Bunn, I can't stop. I've got to catch this paper bag!"

Mr Bunn only heard,

"Bark! Bark! Bark!"

He smiled at Siggy and replied,
"Hi and goodbye, little Siggy!"

But the dachshund
had already
scampered past.

Siggy lolloped on past Marco, the carpenter.
He was wearing his Manchester United shirt.
Marco looked up as he hammered a nail into some wood.
"Hi, Marco!" Siggy called out. "Nice job!"
Marco only heard him say,
"Bark! Bark! Bark!"
Then without looking, he accidentally
banged his thumb with the hammer.

"OUCH!" yelled Marco.

Siggy scampered on, keeping his eyes on the swooping, swirling bag as it flew ahead of him.

He ran past some children playing
on the village swings and roundabout.

They were Hetty, Phoebe and Phyllis.

"Hello, Phyllis!" barked Siggy happily.
"Hello, girls! Can't stop! I'm chasing this paper bag."

"Siggy's funny!" said Hetty.

"Bark! Bark! Bark!"
giggled Phoebe.

"I think he said he's chasing that paper bag!" said Phyllis, who could sometimes understand what Siggy said.

Siggy kept running and soon ran past Vivien, the artist.

"Hello, Vivien!" he said. "Can't stay, in a rush!"

Vivien looked up from her painting.

She heard him perfectly because she was a bit magical and could talk to all the local fairies and sprites too.

"No problem, Siggy," she called.
"Come back later. I'll have some *Hortobagyi* for you."

Siggy loved *Hortobagyi*,
which are pancakes stuffed with all sorts of delicious things that sausage dogs like.

"Sounds yummy!" answered Siggy, but he hurried on after the sparkly paper bag.

He scampered up a mossy bank leading away from the village and into Shady Woods.

Siggy ran under the trees, watching the paper bag fly ahead of him. Then it stopped abruptly as it got caught in some branches high above.

"Oh no!" thought Siggy.

"There is no way I can get the bag now! I'm only a little sausage dog, after all!"

"Hello, Siggy! What are you doing today?" called a familiar voice.

He stopped in his tracks for the first time.

It was Anya, the woodland sprite.
She was Siggy's friend,
and she was full of magic.

Most people wouldn't see Anya, or other fairies and sprites. But Siggy saw her perfectly because doggies can see fairies. When you're walking with your doggie and he seems interested in something that's not really there that's usually because he's saying hello to a fairy. And sometimes children can see them too –
if they believe in magic.

Anya was sitting on one of her favourite blue flowers, near her little house by the red mushrooms.

"I was chasing that paper bag, but now it's stuck in that tree," replied Siggy. "Hello, Anya, how are you today?"

Anya grinned at Siggy.

"I'm *feeling fabulous!"* she laughed.

"I'm going to see Phyllis in a moment. Would you like to come?"

"Usually I would," said Siggy. "But I need to get this bag first! I made a promise."

"Hmmm," said Anya, thinking. "Yes... that bag belongs to Mrs Chana, doesn't it? And you promised to get it for her, didn't you?"

"Yes," Siggy answered.

"Okay," said Anya. "Let me see if I can help."

She took out her tiny wand and chanted something that sounded like:

Paper Bag, come to me
Through the woods and shady trees
Special, sparkly, Paper Bag
Let go the branches, don't you snag
Come to Siggy
Miss that twiggy
Don't make a fuss!
Now, come to us!

The paper bag began to wiggle back and forth in the branches.

It broke free and drifted gently towards Anya,
as if guided by her voice.

Anya caught it in her tiny hands,
and the bag glowed bright white for a few seconds.

"Mrs Chana will be pleased!" Anya beamed,
and she gave the bag to Siggy.

"Thank you!" smiled Siggy. "Now I can take it back."

"Good boy!" said Anya.

"First, here's some Fairy Cake for you too, you clever little sausage."

Siggy's tail wagged very quickly. He loved being called a good boy! And he loved Fairy Cake as well.

Yum! Yum!

Siggy said goodbye to Anya and trotted back toward the village, still enjoying his cake.

Then he began to think about those lovely pancakes Vivien was making.

Yum! Yum!

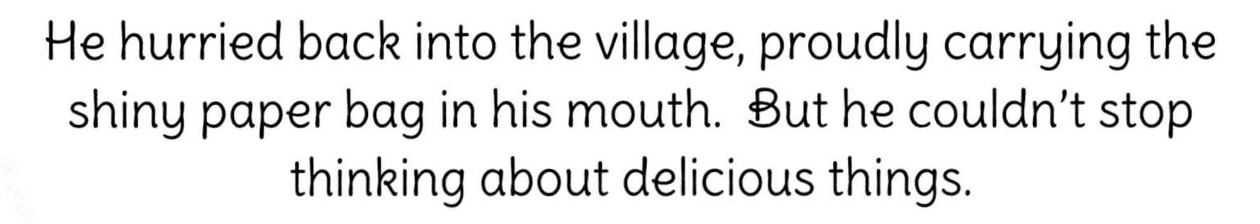

He hurried back into the village, proudly carrying the shiny paper bag in his mouth. But he couldn't stop thinking about delicious things.

And soon he forgot what he was supposed to do with the bag. He stopped to think.

"Oh dear!" Siggy worried, as he paced very slowly.

He saw Marco in his red shirt.

Was he supposed to give the bag to Marco?

He walked past Vivien. Was he supposed to give the bag to Vivien? Siggy didn't think so. He didn't feel like a clever sausage anymore.

"Hello again, Siggy. Are you ready for pancakes?" she asked.

Siggy really did want some pancakes. Yum! Yum! But just then, he remembered what he'd promised to do.

"I'd really love to," he said, "but I have to take this bag back. I promised."

"That's okay," answered Vivien. "See you next time!"

Siggy wagged his tiny tail and scampered off again.

He knew where to go!

As soon as Mrs Chana saw Siggy scurry around the corner, she exclaimed, “Oh, Siggy! You’ve found my bag!

Thank you so much!”

Siggy looked delighted, and his tail wagged even faster.

“Aren’t you clever, Siggy?” laughed Mrs Chana.

She held out her hand, and Siggy scooted up to her with the bag. She was wearing a beautiful Sari, and he loved the way it shone and glittered.

Mrs Chana was a little bit magical too, so she could hear Siggy just like Vivien, Anya and Phyllis could.

"I thought I'd lost this beautiful silk *Chunni* for good," she said, pulling out a headscarf with golden embroidery. "You've saved my daughter's special birthday surprise!"

"Glad to help," said Siggy. "Love the scarf!"

"This makes me so happy! Thank you Siggy." She patted Siggy's head and stroked his soft ears gently.

"Wait here a moment," said Mrs Chana. "You deserve a reward for being such a good boy!"

Siggy beamed. He loved being called a good boy!

Mrs Chana quickly went inside, where she'd been making *Currywurst*, and came out with one of the delicious spicy sausages.

"Who's a good boy?" she cooed, petting the delighted little dog.

"Is it me? Is it me?" asked Siggy excitedly. "It's me, isn't it?"

He wagged his tail so fast, he almost took off like a helicopter!

"Yes," smiled Mrs Chana.

"It IS you!"

She patted him again and gave the tasty sausage
to the little sausage dog. "And this is so spicy, it may
turn you into a hot dog!"

Siggy felt ten feet tall, even though he was only a little dachshund.

He thanked Mrs Chana again and then he swaggered off towards home,
with the yummy sausage in his mouth.

He was feeling very, very happy.

Siggy decided that he liked *Hortobagyi* pancakes, and he adored Fairy Cake, but, apart from keeping promises and helping his friends, there's nothing a sausage dog loves better than sausages.